The Blue Unicorn's Journey To Osm

Coloring Book

by Sybrina Durant

Art by Dasguptarts

Edited by Calyie Martin

"The Blue Unicorn's Journey to Osm" Coloring Book

Story copyright 2016

Soft Cover Print ISBN-13: 978-1537021843 , ISBN-10: 1537021842
Soft Cover Print ISBN-13: 978-1-942740-10-0, ISBN-10: 1-942740-10-7

BISAC Codes:

GAM019000 GAMES / Activity Books (incl. Coloring Books)*
FICTION / General JUV001000
JUV002270   JUVENILE FICTION / Animals / Dragons, Unicorns & Mythical
JUV012030   JUVENILE FICTION / Fairy Tales & Folklore / General
JUV037000   JUVENILE FICTION / Fantasy & Magic
YAF003000 YOUNG ADULT FICTION/ Animals / Mythical Creatures
YAF017000 YOUNG ADULT FICTION / Fairy Tales & Folklore / General
YAF019030 YOUNG ADULT FICTION / Fantasy / Epic

Contact Sybrina@sybrina.com.

Everybody loves unicorns!

Kids. . .Young adults...And many older adults enjoy coloring as a form of meditation or relaxation these days.

This coloring book has been created so that unicorn lovers of all ages can color and learn about all of the unicorns and other characters from the illustrated book, "The Blue Unicorn's Journey To Osm". The colors of the Unicorn bodies, manes and tails are all listed on the descriptive page opposite of each character so use those or make each unicorn uniquely your own.

The beautiful illustrations for the story, by Dasguptarts were painted in water-color. If you decide to try to match that look or if you choose to color with ink that might bleed through the paper, remember to place a piece of cardboard behind the picture first to protect the next page. Crayons, gel pens or colored pencils will not bleed through.

Please share a photo of each of your completed works of art on your Instragram, Pinterest, Facebook and Twitter accounts with #BlueUnicorn in the comment. And like and share our Facebook page https://www.facebook.com/The-Blue-Unicorns-Journey-To-Osm-794155627353303/.

Enjoy the bonus illustrated pages from the book. They give you a little clue of what to expect in the story.

If you'd like to read the story, it is offered in three Versions— An Illustrated Middle Grade Chapter Book, an Illustrated Young Adult Novel and an unillustrated novel. All are available in ebook or print formats at all online book stores.

Learn about other offerings from Sybrina Publishing at www.sybrina.com.

BABY BLUE UNICORN -
Born Without Magic

Horn: Plain Blue Hide-Covered Horn
Body: Light Medium Blue
Mane & Tail: Darker Medium Blue
Hoof: The Walls of his Hooves are Thin But Dense Shiny Horn

Blue is the first unicorn to be born without a metal horn. He is also the first of the Tribe of the Metal Horned Unicorns to possess no magic at his birth. Will he receive magic and save the tribe?

Blue's mother, Miral, has the same blue coloring. Her horn is made of Indium. It's mirrored surface provides a looking glass into other's souls.

Baby Blue Unicorn

And His Mother

THE BLUE UNICORN – He Has No Metal Horn

Horn: Plain Blue Hide-Covered Horn
Body: Light Medium Blue
Mane & Tail: Darker Medium Blue
Hoof: The Walls of his Hooves are Thin But Dense Shiny Horn

His Mate: Ghel, the Golden Horned Unicorn

Blue doesn't feel special because he doesn't have a metal horn and he doesn't have any metal related magical powers. However, as he grows older, he learns he has an adventurous spirit and good old common sense. Will that be enough to save the day in the end for all of the Unicorns?

The Blue Unicorn

As An Adult

GHEL –
The Golden
Horned Unicorn

Herd Crest: Empath—The Empath Herd Crest has an open heart surrounding the Celtic symbol for love.

Horn: Gold

Body: Sweet Clover Honey Colored

Mane & Tail: Blonde

Hoof: The Walls of her Hooves are Gold

Her Mate: Blue, the Plain Blue Unicorn

Ghel is empathic. She senses the emotional levels of those around her.

She loves the Blue Unicorn with all of her heart and can tell that there is a hero inside that plain blue hide. The locket she wears once belonged to Blue's mother.

Ghel

The Golden Horned Unicorn

Iown –
The Iron Horned Unicorn

Herd Crest: Earth Works—
The crest shows a vibrant
flower growing from the
alchemic earth symbol.
Horn: Iron Embedded with
Quartz Crystals
Body: Black Mane & Tail: Dark Gray
Hoof: The Walls of his Hooves are Iron
His Mate: Alumna, the Aluminum Horned Unicorn

Iown is the elder of the tribe and the most intellectual of all the unicorns. He has great insight into the thought processes of others and can help "iron" out their problems. Sometimes he performs acupressure on the third eye of the other unicorns to revive their energy.

Being earth grounded he also possesses the ability to magically revive plants that don't have enough nutrients.

He usually wears a monocle but sometimes he replaces it with a jewelers loupe.

Iown

The Iron Horned Unicorn

Alumna – The Aluminum Horned Unicorn

Herd Crest: Navigator—The symbol for the Navigator Herd is the crystal orb, through which Alumna communicates with the Numen.

Horn: Rubies Encrusted in Her Aluminum Horn

Body: Medium Red   Mane & Tail: Dark Red.

Hoof: The Walls of her Hooves are Aluminum

Her Mate: Iown, the Iron Horned Unicorn

Alumna is the Oracle of the Metal Horned Unicorn Tribe. She receives messages from Numen, the Moon Star Spirit, through a crystal orb. She misses most of what he says because there is a bad connection with a lot of static. It is her duty to reveal his words to the other unicorns.

She usually wears an oracle hat with a tassel.

Alumna

The Aluminum Horned Unicorn

Cornum - The Brass Horned Unicorn

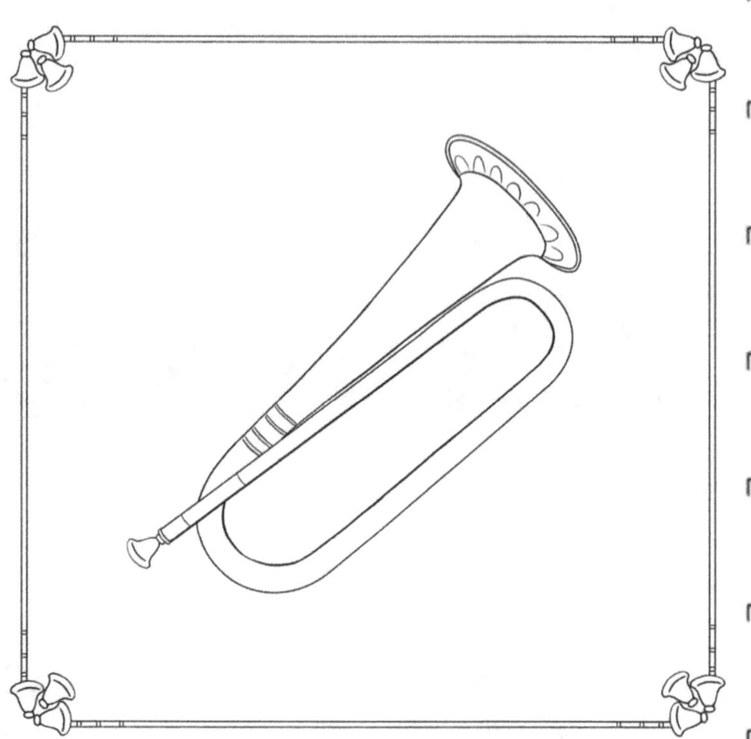

Herd Crest: Musician—The brass bugle is the symbol for the Musician Herd Crest.

Horn: Brass— This is the only unicorn horn with a Flared Tip.

Body: Dark Yellowish Green Mane: Light Yellowish Green

Hoof: The Walls of his Hooves are Brass

His Mate: Style, the Steel Horned Unicorn

His magical talent is music. His horn actually acts as a brass instrument so it can sound like a trumpet, trombone, tuba or any other brass wind instrument. Sometimes Style decorates his mane with lemons and limes, which he doesn't like. She got the idea from all the sour notes that blast from his horn when he's perturbed. His parents were a copper horned filly and a zinc horned stallion which is where he got his brass alloy horn.

Cornum

The Brass Horned

Unicorn

Style -
The Steel
Horned Unicorn

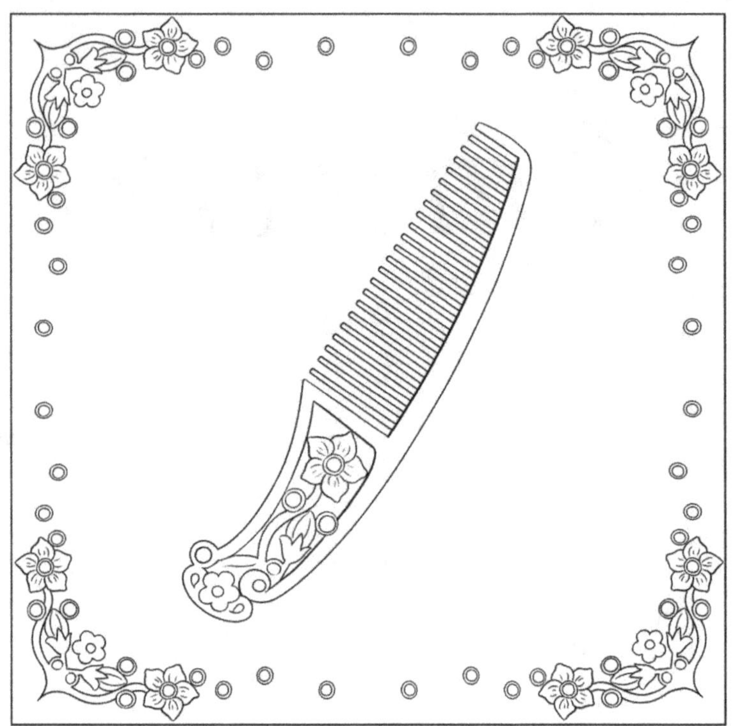

Herd Crest: Stylest—The Stylest Herd symbol is a steel comb engraved with a pretty ornament.

Horn: Steel Embedded with Amethysts

Body: Medium Purple   Mane & Tail: Dark Purple

Hoof: The Walls of her Hooves are Steel

Her Mate: Cornum, the Brass Horned Unicorn

Style runs the Groomane Salon. It is the beauty parlor and fitness center for the other unicorns. Her magical ability is to style the other unicorns manes and to decorate their hooves with the touch of her horn.

She likes to keep herself in shape and she loves all of the latest fashions in leggings. Her motto is: When you look good, you feel good, too.

Style

The Steel

Unicorn

Nix –
The Nickel
Horned Unicorn

Herd Crest: Defender—A
lightning bolt is the symbol
for the Defender Herd.
Horn: Nickel
Body: Light Gray   Mane & Tail: Dark Gray
Hoof: The Walls of his Hooves are Nickel
His Mate: Silubhra, the Silver Horned Unicorn

Nix's magical talent is that he can sense when another member of the tribe is in trouble. When that happens, the air fills with sparkles as he disappears, to magically reappear in the nick of time to rescue them. Blue is the only member of the tribe that Nix can not detect.

His horn is so powerful that it can blast through rocks or even

The Nickel
Horned Unicorn

Silubhra - The Silver Horned Unicorn

Herd Crest: Communications—A Musical staff and smiling lips adorn the crest of the Communications Herd.

Horn: Silver Embedded with Diamonds

Body: White

Mane & Tail: Metallic Silver

Hoof: The Walls of her Hooves are Silver

Her Mate: Nix, the Nickel Horned Unicorn

Silubhra is the silver-tongued unicorn. Her soothing voice is magical to hear and it can be very persuasive to any listener.

Sometimes her mane is decorated with baby's breath and her hooves are painted with butterflies.

Silubhra

The Silver Horned Unicorn

Dr. Zinko –
The Zinc Horned Unicorn

Herd Crest: Medical—The Medical Herd is represented by a stethoscope with a unicorn shape in the tube.

Horn: Zinc

Body: White

Mane & Tail: Medium Blue

Hoof: The Walls of his Hooves are Zinc

His Mate: Lauda, the Lead Horned Unicorn

Dr. Zinko's metal magic gives him a healing power so that also makes him the doctor of the tribe. Each time he has to use his magic to heal another unicorn, he gives a little bit of himself away.

Dr.
Zinko

The Zinc

Horned Unicorn

Lauda – The Lead Horned Unicorn

Herd Crest: Scientist—The Scientific Herd symbol is a potion bottle.

Horn: Lead

Body: Dark Gray

Mane & Tail: Light Gray

Hoof: The Walls of her Hooves are Lead

Her Mate: Dr. Zinko, the Zinc Horned Unicorn

Lauda is a scientist who can create potions and elixirs by swirling her lead horn in liquids or powders.

She is also the caretaker of the outer shell of the Halstable. She can repair fissures in the metal surface with a touch of her horn.

Lauda

The Lead

Horned Unicorn

Tinam –
The Tin Horned
Unicorn

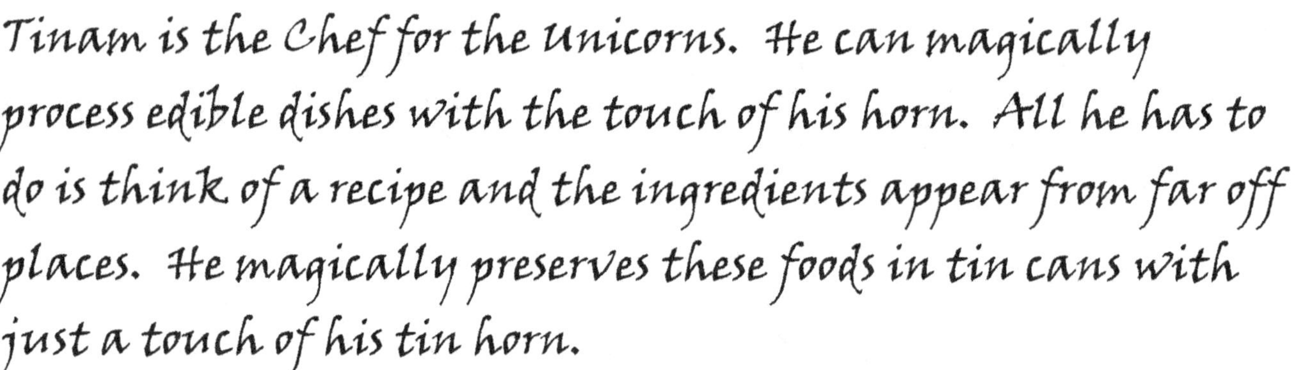

Herd Crest: Chef—The toque or chef's hat is the symbol on the Herd Crest of the unicorn chefs.

Horn: Tin

Body: Light Yellow   **Mane & Tail:** Lemon Yellow

Hoof: The Walls of his Hooves are Tin

His Mate: Cuprum, the Copper Horned Unicorn

Tinam is the Chef for the Unicorns. He can magically process edible dishes with the touch of his horn. All he has to do is think of a recipe and the ingredients appear from far off places. He magically preserves these foods in tin cans with just a touch of his tin horn.

When another unicorn taps one of these tins with their horn, the lid rolls back revealing a piping hot delicious meal.

Tinam
The Tin
Horned Unicorn

Cuprum - The Copper Horned Unicorn

Herd Crest: Water—. The Water Purification Herd Crest shows a copper cup with the alchemy symbol for water emblazoned on it.

Horn: Copper Embedded with Emeralds

Body: Dark Green   Mane & Tail: Red With Green Streaks - Being copper, it sometimes looks tarnished.

Hoof: The Walls of her Hooves are Copper

Her Mate: Tinam, the Copper Horned Unicorn

Cuprum is a scientist who's abilities allow her to purify water so that the tribe always has fresh water to drink.

With her magical horn, she can create clean water from any source, including mud puddles and the ocean. She also creates water purification pebbles for the others to use when she is not around.

Cuprum

The Copper Horned Unicorn

Osm - The Unicorn With The Multi-metal Horn

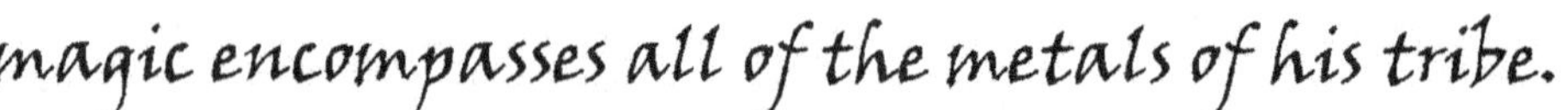

Herd Crest: Pilot—A metal wand was the symbol for the Pilot Herd but Osm's is multi-metal because his magic encompasses all of the metals of his tribe.

Horn: Platinum base with twelve different types of metal spiraling around it. It is tipped with Osmium

Body: Dark Blue   Mane & Tail: Many Shades of Blue

Feather: Azure   Hoof: The Walls of his Hooves are Osmium

His Mate: Ghel, the Golden Horned Unicorn

The Blue Unicorn becomes Osm at the end of his quest. When he transforms he has a shining horn with 12 different types of metal braiding in a spiral up towards the sky.

On its spear tip is shining blue Osmium, the most impenetrable of all metals. Osmium is coveted by Magh, the evil sorcerer.

The Unicorn With The Multi-Metal Horn

Other Characters From The Book

The Manticore

They are the most fearsome predator of the unicorns. They have a Head of a Man, Body of a Lion, Bat-like Wings and Tail of a Dragon tipped with a Scorpion's Stinger. Fresh unicorn meat is this carnivore's favorite tasty treat. They are on constant lookout for unicorns for the evil sorcerer, Magh. They play the role of Magh's brutish henchmen and they have no mercy for their victims.

Manticore are too heavy to fly but they can glide when they leap from high spaces. They move swiftly and quietly on padded paws, attacking their victims with very little warning.

THE BUZZY-BITER loves the nectar of the Jughead bush.

He spends a lot of time there buzzing from flower to flower.

When the Blue Unicorn unwarily swats at him with his tail, Buzzy becomes quite annoyed and retaliates by zeroing in on Blue's rump with his stinger.

The stinger grows back immediately but Buzzy-Biter venom is nearly fatal to some unicorns. Blue is strongly affected by the poison.

Medical assistance is required and soon!

Buzzy-Biter

THREE CUSSERS FROM EGADA

Blue nervously watches as these most unpleasant chaps approach his home, the Halstable.

Unwittingly, they narrowly miss the cloaked compound by making a sharp right turn just before reaching the entrance.

The entire time, they are cussing and quarrelling with each other, completely oblivious to the magical creatures living inside the invisible structure.

The Cussers were once friends of the unicorns but they are now under Magh's binding spell and do his bidding.

Three Cussers

From Egada

PIDO AND FLEOGE are Fairies in the Guarded Forest

They are friendly with all the unicorn of the Tribe of the Metal Horn.

The two playful fairies are brother and sister who live in the Guarded Forest. Blue has spent a lot of time playing tag with them to sharpen his eye-sight and increase his ability to zig and zag with ease while running.

They try to help the Blue Unicorn gain information to make his quest easier.

Pido
and
Fleoge

WAAP the OPOSSUM lives in the Guarded Forest

Pido and Fleoge seek advice from him in behalf of the Blue Unicorn but he's not interested in talking.

He just wants to sleep.

Waap

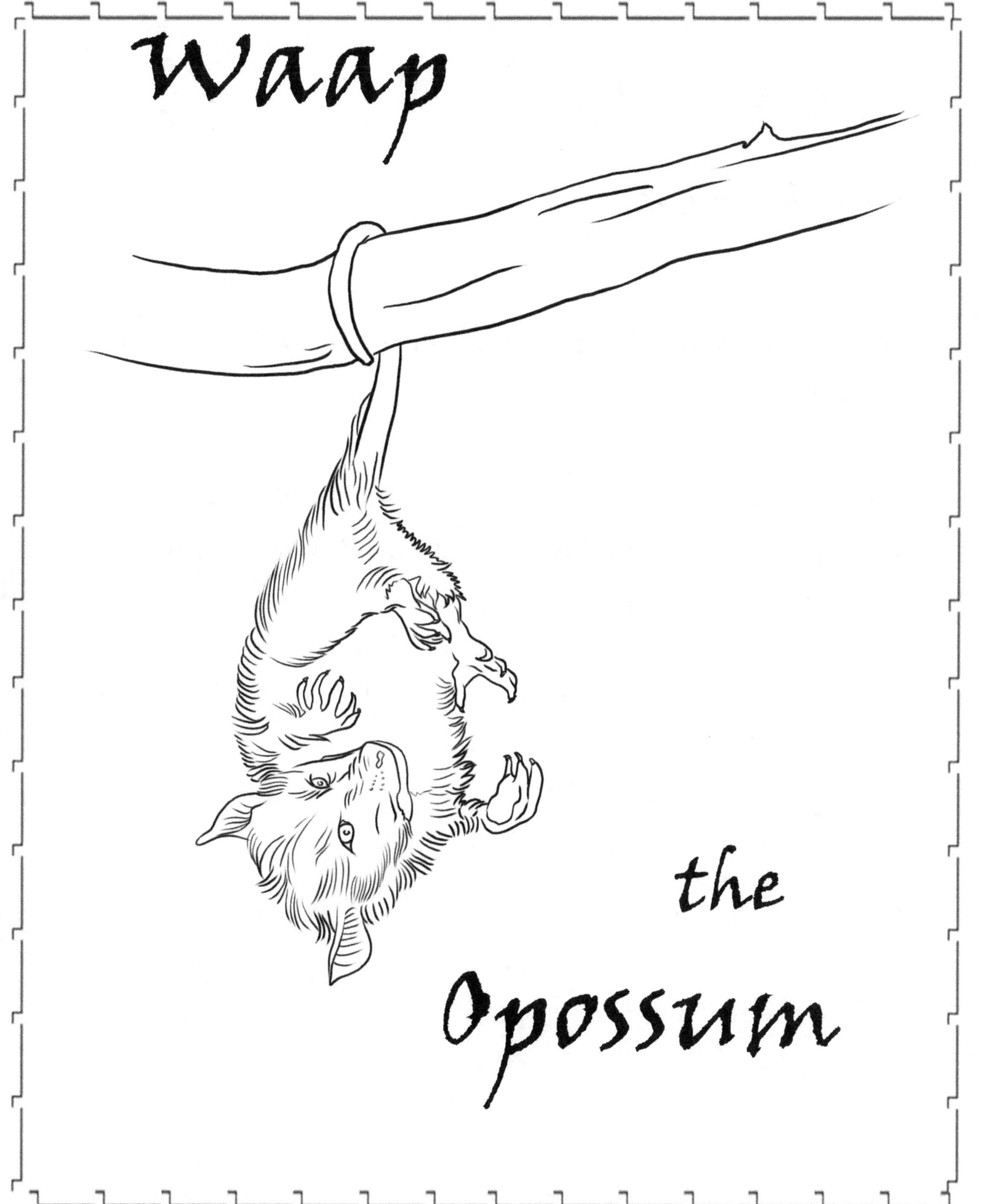

the

Opossum

OURA and OLINA live in the Guarded Forest

They are a couple of cute little brown squirrels with big bushy tails.

They are known to keep their paws on the pulse of the entire forest so the Blue Unicorn consults with them while in the Guarded Forest.

Oura

and

Olina

Gaiso and Springen in the Guarded Forest

Gaiso is an impressive-looking buck with a coat of deep red and a white beard. On his head is a fifteen point rack, at least seven feet from point to point. Magnificent, aptly describes the stag, who is easily as tall as Blue. He makes the perfect travelling companion for the blue unicorn.

His sister, Springen is a small spotted doe with a sweet temperament that reminds Blue of Ghel, the Gold Horned Unicorn.

Gaiso, the Stag

and

Springen, a Doe

GIRASOL, THE FIREBIRD

has bright scarlet and orange plumage.

When she beats her wings very rapidly, fire is conjured. Her name, Girasol, means fire-opal, a stone with brilliant flame-like colors. Her diet consists of Pepo seeds. Under normal circumstances a single seed gives her vitality for five days but her exertions to help Blue Requires her to eat more often.

She helps guide Blue from the air during his travels.

Her motto is: Never leave a friend behind.

Girasol

The Firebird

LEDER, THE HUMONGAS ELUTRON is a

humongous gentle bug, hunted for the leather material covering its wings.

The stiff leathery stuff is used to make shoes and shields because it is so tough. The filmy stuff of his under-wings is used for scarves and veils by the Bugans, a ghastly crew of bug-bashers from Bugansville.

Blue, Gaiso and Girasol must save the poor beetle from certain death. Leder promises to repay them for their kindness.

Leder

The Humongas Elutron

The Bugans

These three Bugans live near the Phlat Plains in Bugansville. They hunt the Hunongas Elutron to make shields from their leathery wings. They also prize the filmy under-wings of the Elutron for crafting scarves and veils. After cutting off their wings, they leave the Elutrons defenseless to die on the plain.

They are a brutal society whose lives are spent hunting and slaughtering. They are happy to do the dirty work for the evil sorcerer, Magh.

Their favorite delicacy is Pendragon eggs.

The

Bugans

GWYN THE PENDRAGON has been trapped in the Heptagonos Valley by Yegwa, the Spirit of Eternal Spring.

She has the face of a dragon with a penguin's beak, two webbed feet and little tiny flightless flipper wings that are red. Her body has short furry feathers and are white on her underbelly. The rest of her body is black. Her dragon tail is tipped with long red and green feathers.

Girasol, the Firebird, saves Gwyn, Blue and Gaiso from the Yegwa. Gwyn then travels with the group until they reach her friend, Icel, the Ice Blink at the top of the world.

Gywn

The Pendragon

MAGH THE SORCERER from Kudos has nothing

but evil intentions for unicorns.

He uses their horns and hooves to create magical potions for conquering the inhabitants of the land of MarBryn. Over the centuries, his soldiers have captured and killed all the Metal Horned Unicorns except for the twelve remaining members.

It will be up to the Blue Unicorn to try to save them all.

Magh

The Sorcerer

The Mauve Unicorn

Was unlucky enough to find herself alone in a forest, trapped by a Manticore.

Centuries ago, when Magh was a young apprentice sorcerer from the small town of Jeribild, he stumbled across them.

Jenin, as he was named then, vanquished the manticore through strength borne of sheer terror but he also accidentally killed the unicorn.

What happened next turned him into the evil sorcerer who became the scourge of the land of MarBryn.

The Mauve

Unicorn

Kata — BATTALION COMMANDER—Kudos Warrior from the Lethean Silva

The warrior tribe of Kudos was a brave and honorable race from the Lethean Silva before being forced into Magh's Infantry Corps. Except for very few, most were completely under the thrall of the magician's binding spells.

The Battalion Commander is not as susceptible to Magh's power as others in her clan but she does as he bids since it is in her best interest to do so. She hopes the time will come when she might be able to break her people away from the vile overlord.

Kata—Kudos

Warrior

Battalion Commander

IMROZ THE RAGAMOFFYN *from the Red Band of Weita.*

As a child, Imroz was abducted by Magh's warriors and brought back to Kudos to be pressed into the evil magician's servantry corps. Magh paid no attention to her as she was of such a lowly station. This near invisibility allowed her to secretly observe him when he practiced magic.

Over time, with much trial and error, she became proficient in mastering some of his minor skills. Little by little she stole various potions in the hope that one day, she'd be able to use them to help, rather than harm the unicorns.

When the Metal Horned Tribe wandered into Kudos, she found her perfect opportunity.

Imroz

Ragamoffyn from the
Red Band of Weita

LETHEAN WARRIORS—In Magh, The Sorcerer's Infantry Corps

Most of these warriors are in the thrall of the evil sorcerer, Magh. He uses binding spells and potions to force them to do his bidding.

Very few are able to resist. These three can but they simply enjoy doing his dirty work.

Lethean Warriors

Infantry Corps

THE BLIND BLOBER lives in the Caulis Caverns under the Barricad Mountains.

The poor thing is a big, fat, sullen, lumpy, blobby creature with antenna where his eyes should be. He can't shed tears but he sobs all the time, "Uh-hoomp, uh--haump, uh-hump. Booo-hooo-hooo." He's got a big mouth, big enough to eat a unicorn, but he doesn't have teeth. He just gums his occasional victims to death.

When the Tribe of the Metal Horn bump into him in the Caulis Caverns, they barely escape with their lives!

The Blind

Blober

The Ice Blink Lives at the top of the world in the Smaul Mountains.

The big guy may be ice bound to the mountain but that doesn't mean he is totally isolated from communicating with others. He communicates with the Moon-Star Numen via crystals and copper deposits deep below the mountain. They act as transmitters and receivers from the depths of space and all across the land of MarBryn.

When Blue and his companions stop by for a visit, he enlightens the unicorn about the origins of his ancestors.

The Ice Blink

Icel

BAB THE NEBUL AND PICI THE WOODTHUMPER from Muzika Woods

Nebuls are a tribe of musical communicators who sing their words. They are a gentle race whose bodies are so misty that you can almost see through them. Bab plays the Rebec, a pear-shaped, 3 stringed instrument. All Nebuls have an animal harmonizer to enhance their music.

Bab's is Pici, a bird which resembles a woodpecker with a stiff tail that it props itself back on as it makes drum like sounds by pecking its beak on hollow wood.

Bab explains to Blue that he must enter the Nebulium Circle in order to receive the knowledge of the Moon Star.

Bab the Nebul

and

Pici

The

Woodthumper

MONKEN THE NEBUL AND HIS HARMONIZER, HOULEN *from Muzika Woods*

Monken's musical instrument is the Hurda-Gurda which is a pear-shaped string instrument played by turning a crank on the side.

His harmonizer is Houlen, which is a small monkey like creature with a very long tail. It makes mild howling sounds to accompany the Hurda-Gurda.

Monken
and
Houlen

SALLIEN THE NEBUL AND CITA, HER HARMONIZER from Muzika Woods

Sallien's musical instrument is the Psaltery, which is a harp like affair played by plucking strings. The Psaltery travels from one place to another under its own power.

Her harmonizer is Cita, a very small cat that looks like a Cheeta with very long legs. It plucks the bottom strings for her.

Sallien
and
Cita

Some Places From The Book

Icy Cold Lake

Home
of

The Cubose

The Tribe of the Metal Horned Unicorns and The Blue Unicorn's group of travelers make separate stops at the Icy Cold Lake where they meet the Cubose. The Cubose are manufactured by the Ice Blink.

THE SINGING TREES OF MUZIKA WOOD have leaves that sound like wind chimes as the wind caresses them.

Sometimes, the trees sing along with the Nebuls who live in their enchanted forest. And when the wind blows through the hollows in their trunks, it makes a droning sound like, "didjerry, didjerry, didjerry." Their musical symphony can be mesmerizing.

The Singing Trees
of

Muzika Wood

THE HALSTABLE is the Home of the Metal Horned Unicorns

It is the unicorn's hide-away because it is invisible to every other creature. With magical spells all around its perimeter, others just walk around without even bumping into it. The Halstable is set right in the center of a beautiful U-shaped valley by a large lake fed by waterfalls. Numen, the Moon-Star Spirit brought the Halstable to earth.

Each unicorn couple has their own apartment plus special areas set up for each unicorn's special craft or personality. The Great Room is where they all eat and play indoor games. It also contains Tinam's Kitchen.

Other areas include: Style's Groomane Salon & Fitness Center, Lauda and Cuprum's Scientific Laboratory, Dr. Zinko's Medical Facilities, Cornum and Silubhra's Music Conservatory, Ghel and Iown's Psychology Center and Alumna's Sanctuary of the Oracle.

The Halstable - Home of The

Metal Horned Unicorns

THE MAP

Shows two paths. Blue Unicorn and his companions travel in their journey to Muzika Woods. Blue meets up with Gaiso, the stag in the Guarded Forest. Then, in the Phlat Plains, Girasol the Firebird joins the unicorn and the stag. Blue and Gaiso meet Gwyn, the Pendragon in the 7 Sided Heptagonos Valley. Everyone except Girasol becomes enchanted there by Yegwa, the spirit of Eternal Spring.

The Firebird saves them and they flee through the Rainbow Colored Bands of Weita on their way to the Smaul Mountains. First they pass the Icy Cold lake and meet the Cubose. Then, they visit with Icel, the Ice Blink at the top of the world. Finally, the travelling companions make it to their destination of Muzika Woods.

The dashed line shows the route that the Tribe of the Metal Horned Unicorns take to reach the Muzika Woods. They leave the Halstable in search of someone who can tell them how to get to their destination. Magh's, City of Kudos.

OF MarBryn

They stop in the first city they come to which happens to be the evil Sorcerer, Magh's, City of Kudos.

They are helped by a little Ragamoffyn named Imroz but Magh's soldiers are in hot pursuit. The tribe finally loses them at the entrance of the Caulis Caverns. They have an encounter with the Blind Blober deep inside the caverns. They escape through the Lickety Split and find their way to the Icy Cold Lake where the Firebird finds them. Girasol guides the tribe to Muzika Woods in time for the arrival of the Moon Star.

Other places of note on the map are 1) Egada, where the Cussers live, 2) Lethean Silva, where Magh's Warriors originated, 3) Manticore Domain in the Kinubalu Desert, where Nix and Ghel encounter a Manticore, 4) the Village of Jeribild, where many of Magh's servants are from and finally, 5) Muzika Woods, home of the Nebuls and their Harmonizers.

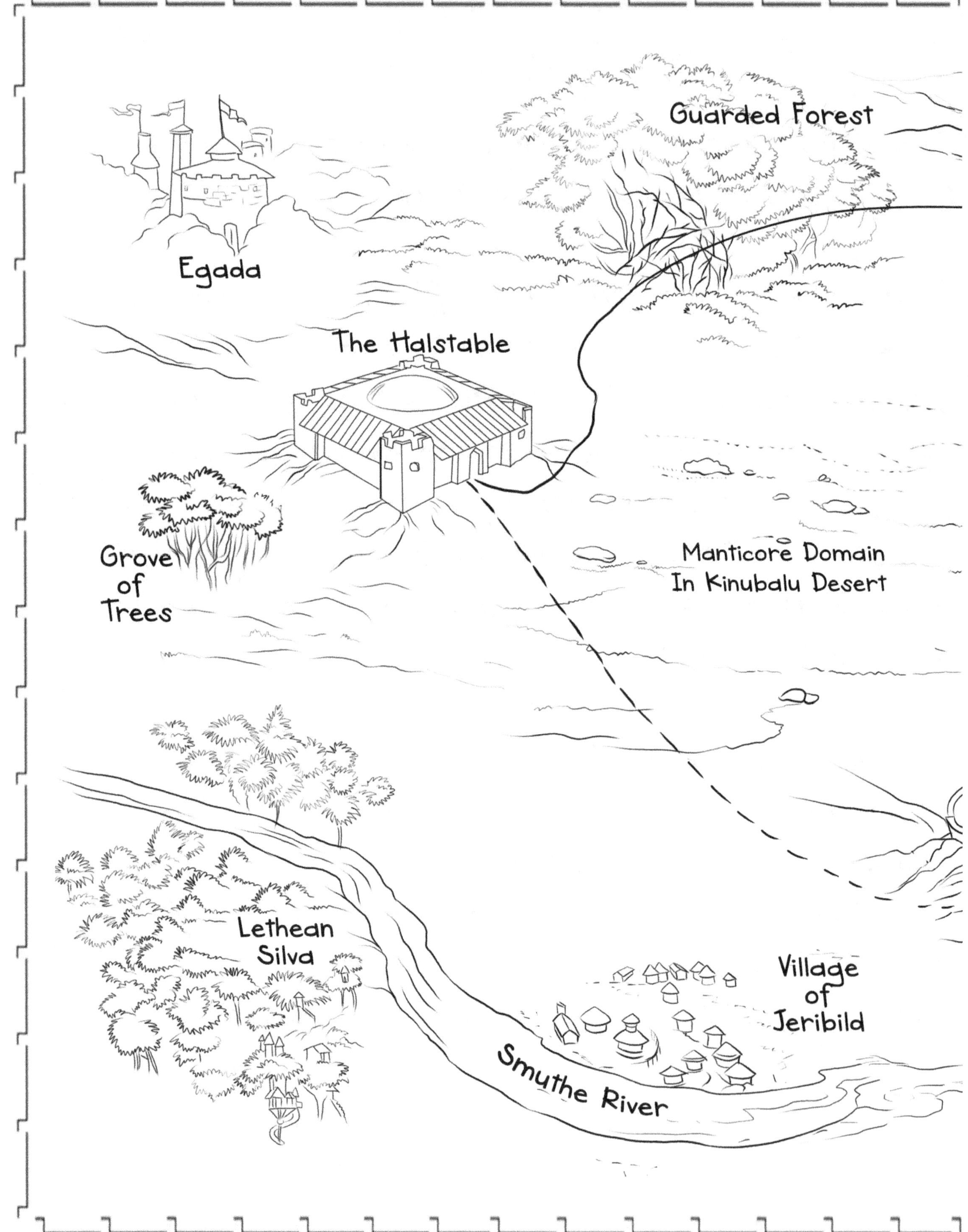

Egada
Guarded Forest
The Halstable
Grove
of
Trees
Manticore Domain
In Kinubalu Desert
Lethean
Silva
Village
of
Jeribild
Smuthe River

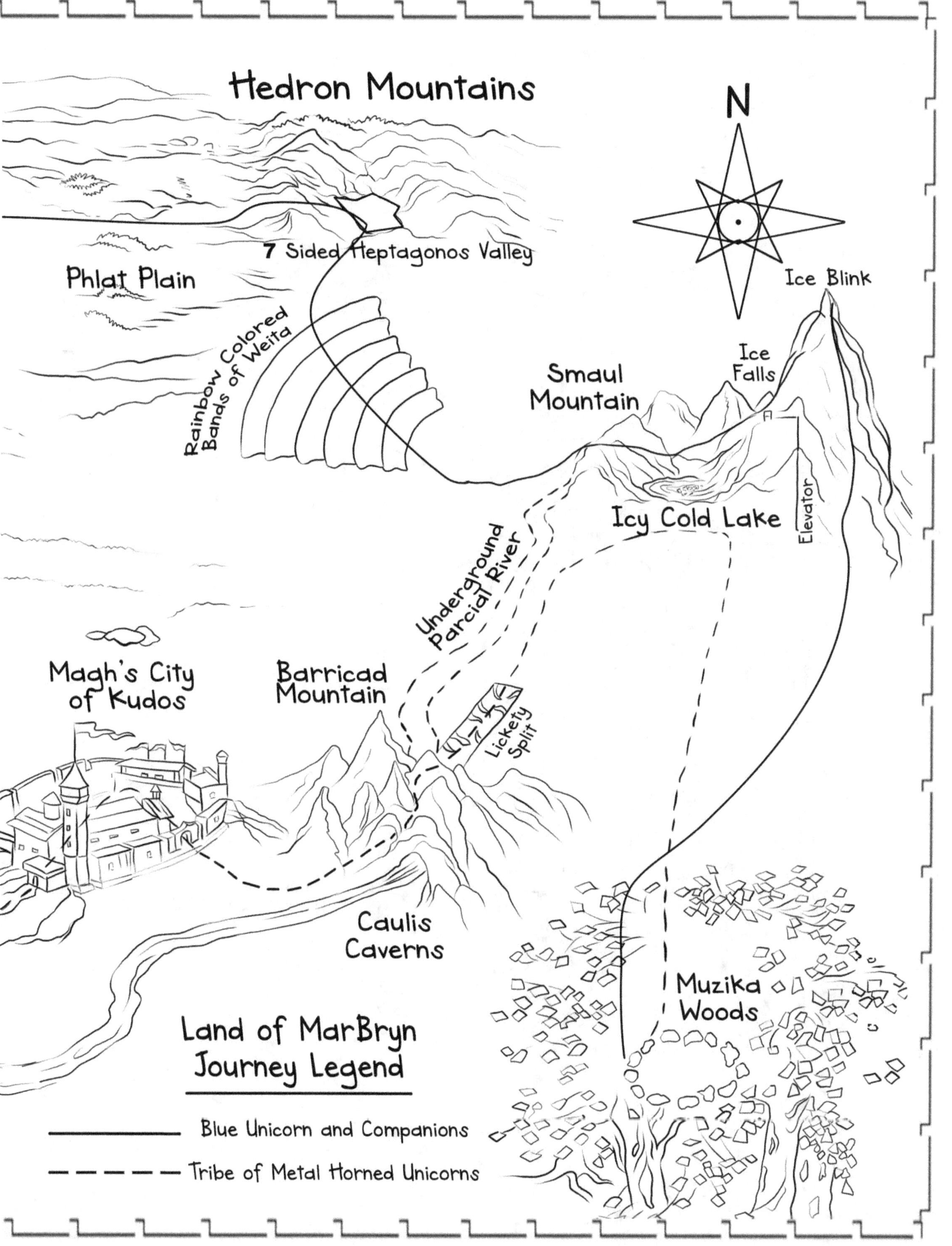

Hedron Mountains
N
Phlat Plain
7 Sided Heptagonos Valley
Ice Blink
Rainbow Colored Bands of Weita
Smaul Mountain
Ice Falls
Underground Parcial River
Icy Cold Lake
Elevator
Magh's City of Kudos
Barricad Mountain
Lickety Split
Caulis Caverns
Muzika Woods
Land of MarBryn Journey Legend
Blue Unicorn and Companions
Tribe of Metal Horned Unicorns

Here's
A
Peek
At
The
Illustrated
Novel

Prologue

Long Ago IN THE FARAWAY LAND OF OF MARBRYN, A MAGICAL creature was born.   The Tribe of Metal Horned Unicorns had gathered to behold his horn and observe his magic.

The frail little foal didn't look very impressive. Why, he didn't even have metal horn! This little blue unicorn's horn was covered with a plain blue velvety hide. Not a glint of metal to be seen. No metal meant no magic.

All the other unicorns came into the world with bright, shiny, metal horns endowed with magical properties unique to the metal of its particular herd. The baby's own mother had a horn that showed the other unicorns their reflections in its soft silvery veneer. The magic of her indium horn also let her see right into another's soul.

Alumna, the aluminum horned unicorn oracle of the tribe looked at the puny looking little thing in despair. The prophecy from the Moon-Star Spirit had led her to expect a stronger looking foal.

"Did I misunderstand what the Numen was trying to show me?" she wondered. *"This little unicorn could never save the tribe…could he?"* It seemed unfair for the pitiful little foal to be saddled with such a burden at birth.

"Oh Miral, I'm so sorry," the rose colored mare tried to console the little foal's mother. "Maybe his magic will present itself later. You mustn't give up hope."

"Do you really think so, Alumna?" The anguished new mother's voice rose and fell as hope and despair wrestled in a battle that wouldn't be won that day.

Alumna wasn't sure what to think so she didn't respond.

Miral peered at her son through big teardrops welling in her eyes. She tapped his forehead with her Indium horn, wishing she could transfer her own magic to him. Its mirrored surface captured silvery blue moonlight for a brief instant and she caught a flickering image of a magnificent multi-hued blue stallion rearing up as if in some kind of triumph. But there was no change in her little one's hide covered horn.

She looked up to the sky, crying out with a heavy heart, *"What is to become of my poor little unicorn? What will become of the Tribe of the Metal Horn?"*

If you enjoyed learning about the characters in "The Blue Unicorn's Journey to Osm" in this Coloring Book, then you might be interested in reading one (or all) of the three different versions of the story.

The three versions are an Illustrated Middle Grade Chapter Book, an Illustrated Young Adult Novel and an un-illustrated novel. The illustrated stories contain forty full color fun packed pictures.

Purchase them all in ebook or print formats at all online book stores. Look for audio versions of the books sometime soon, too.

Visit Sybrina.com for more info.

Sybrina Publishing

Where You'll Find Children's Picture Books and More

These books are available in print and Ebook formats at all online book stores.
Ask for them at your local library and your favorite brick and mortar book stores.
For discount price information contact Sybrina@sybrina.com.

Books For Boys

Learn To Tie Books

Books For Girls

Other Books From

Sybrina Publishing

All of these books have accompanying songs. Listen to them for FREE at
http://www.Sybrina.com.